Published by Ladybird Books Ltd
A Penguin Company
Penguin Books Ltd, 80 Strand, London, WC2R 0RL, England
Penguin Books Australia Ltd, Camberwell, Victoria, Australia
Penguin Group (NZ), cnr Airborne and Rosedale Roads, Albany,
Auckland 1310, New Zealand

ISBN-13: 978-1-84646-124-8
ISBN-10: 1-8464-6124-3

Manufactured in Italy

Two Mice in a Boat

It was bedtime but Angelina wasn't tired. She'd found her father's old Miller's Pond Boat Carnival trophy. "Oh Dad! I'm determined to win this year," she said.

"And how are you going to decorate your boat, Angelina?" asked her father. "Well," began Angelina. "It will be a huge white swan, with gold thrones for Alice and me, the Swan Princesses!" "It sounds lovely dear, but don't count on being teamed with Alice," warned Mrs Mouseling gently.

The next day at school, Miss Chalk announced the boat decorating teams. "Priscilla with Penelope, Flora with William, Angelina with Sammy . . ."

"Sammy!" said Angelina, shocked.

"Angelina!" spluttered Sammy.

"Alice with Henry," continued Miss Chalk. Alice looked horrified.

"It's all about teamwork!" said Miss Chalk over the din of unhappy mice.

Angelina and Sammy lined up to collect their boat from Captain Miller.

"I wouldn't be seen dead in a sissy swan boat," muttered Sammy.

"Well, you wouldn't catch me on some stupid pirate ship!" spat Angelina.

"We're never going to agree," sighed Angelina, looking at Sammy's plans. "So we'll just have to try and . . .

"Work together," they both muttered.

The next day, they drew a line down the middle of the boat. They decided to decorate one half each. "Don't go over the line," warned Angelina sternly. "Don't worry, I won't!" said Sammy.

Just along the river, Alice and Henry were decorating their boat with sweets. "One for the boat, one for you!" they said in turn happily, popping sweets into each other's mouths.

On the day of the carnival, Angelina and
Sammy got ready early and went to try
out their boat on the river.
"It floats!" cried Angelina, when they
eventually managed to launch it.

The two mice turned round when they heard a rumbling noise behind them. It was the builder mouse, Mr Ratchett.

"Nice boat you've got there!" he said. "What's she called?"
"The Swan Princess," said Angelina.
"The Pirate King," shouted Sammy.
"That's a big name for a small boat!" chuckled Mr Ratchett as he carried on up the road.

The mouselings jumped on board.
"I think we're sinking," said Sammy, as
he watched water seeping into the boat.
"I said that cannon was too heavy!" cried
Swan Princess Angelina, furiously.
"It's that stupid bird's head, more like,"
muttered Pirate Sammy.

They began to throw things out of the
boat as fast as they could, until there
was absolutely nothing left.

"We're floating now!" said Sammy.
"Downstream!" shouted Angelina
desperately. "Where are the oars?"
"Over there!" cried Sammy, pointing to
the oars floating between the cannon
and the swan's head.

Meanwhile, Alice and Henry had nearly
finished their boat, even though they'd
spent quite a lot of time eating the
decorations and felt a little sick!

Further upstream, Angelina and Sammy
were moving fast!
"We've got to stop!" yelled Angelina.
"I can see a tree stump up ahead!"
bellowed Sammy.
"We need some rope to loop over it.
Look!" Angelina had seen something.
"Vines!" They both said together.

As the little boat sped along, the two
frightened mice grabbed onto the vines.

"Puuuull!" screamed Sammy.
The vines broke away from the bank
and Angelina found the longest one.
They grabbed one end each just as the
boat reached the tree stump.

They struggled to loop it over the stump and pulled themselves onto the bank. "We have to get back to Miller's Pond!" said a desperate Angelina.
They heard a chug chug behind them.
"Mr Ratchett!" they both said, relieved.

At Miller's Pond, the Carnival was underway. Alice and Henry were dressed as lollipops and their boat was decorated entirely with sweet papers!

Suddenly there was a distant chugging noise and everybody turned to look.
It was Swan Princess Angelina and Pirate Sammy. They were floating along in the sky, on the end of Mr Ratchett's crane!

Everyone at Miller's Pond clapped and cheered as they were slowly lowered towards the water.

SPLASH! They landed a bit too close
to Priscilla and Penelope Pinkpaws'
boat. It was decorated as a huge pink
ballet shoe. "Our lovely shoe!" they
squeaked. "Now it's soaking wet."
Angelina and Sammy giggled together.

"The winners are Alice and Henry," said
Captain Miller a little later.
"But this year's prize for teamwork goes
to Angelina and Sammy!"

Mr Mouseling introduced Angelina to
his old boating partner – Sammy's dad!
"We never won a teamwork prize," said
Mr Watts. "We were always arguing."
"No we weren't!" replied Mr Mouseling.

Angelina and Sammy giggled.
"YOU keep the trophy," said Angelina.
"No, you keep it," replied Sammy.

The two mouselings, and their fathers,
carried on arguing and laughing until
the sun went down and it was time for
every tired mouse to go home to bed.